BETTER TOGETHER

BETTER TOGETHER

Sheryl and Simon Shapiro

Illustrated by
Dušan Petričić

annick press
toronto + new york + vancouver

Annick Press Ltd.
All rights reserved. No part of this work covered by the copyrights hereon may be reproduced or used in any form or by any means – graphic, electronic, or mechanical – without the prior written permission of the publisher.

We acknowledge the support of the Canada Council for the Arts, the Ontario Arts Council, and the Government of Canada through the Canada Book Fund (CBF) for our publishing activities.

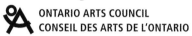

ONTARIO ARTS COUNCIL
CONSEIL DES ARTS DE L'ONTARIO

Cataloging in Publication

Shapiro, Sheryl
        Better together / Sheryl and Simon Shapiro ; illustrated by Dušan Petričić.

ISBN 978-1-55451-279-9 (bound).—ISBN 978-1-55451-278-2 (pbk.)

        1. Combinations—Juvenile poetry.
I. Shapiro, Simon II. Petričić, Dušan III. Title.

PS8637.H368B47 2011   jC811'.6   C2010-907470-X

For Stephen and Anne, happy together.
—S.S. and S.S.

For Tia, the smart girl from Novi Sad.
—D.P.

Distributed in Canada by:
Firefly Books Ltd.
66 Leek Crescent
Richmond Hill, ON
L4B 1H1

Published in the U.S.A. by Annick Press (U.S.) Ltd.
Distributed in the U.S.A. by:
Firefly Books (U.S.) Inc.
P.O. Box 1338
Ellicott Station
Buffalo, NY 14205

Printed in China

Visit us at: www.annickpress.com

MIXTURES

You take two things, or three or four,
or even five or six.
You stir and squoosh them, squish and moosh them,
mingle, blend, and mix.

And as you jumble, magically,
they disappear from sight.
And in their place, instead, appears
a brand new thing. Delight!

CONCRETE

We stopped to watch the mixer
sloshing 'round the sand,
gravel, water, and cement,
and now I understand.

Concrete starts all soft and slushy
then gets hard—that's clever.
Just the sort of thing to keep
our footprints here forever.

FUDGE

The sugar melts like magic
when stirred with heated milk.
Add butter to the puddle—
get fudge as smooth as silk.

The cooling fudge needs testing.
I'll taste a lick or two.
Another . . .
and another . . .
Oh no! There's none for you!

GLUE

To stick two things together
if you don't have any glue,
you can take some soft white flour
and a splash of water, too.

Then mix them, squish them, squoosh them
'til you get a sticky goo.
But be careful how you use it,
or some stuff could stick to you!

CINNAMON TOAST

Peanut butter's boring.
Jam's the same old thing.
Honey's much too sticky.
Banana's got no zing.

Cinnamon tastes funny.
Sugar's much too sweet.
But mix those two and add to toast—
delicious! What a treat!

MUSIC

We've got Caitlin on the kettle drum,
Gary strums guitar.
Pia pounds the piano,
and Shelly shakes the jar.

We rock and roll together,
banging four beats to the bar,
and I'm the leader of the band,
so I will be the star!

17

BUBBLES

Puppy's very dirty.
How to get her clean?
Swish and swash her in the washer?
No! That would be mean!

Rub and scrub with soap and water,
watch the bubbles fly.
Splash! The towel got soaking wet.
Can we spin her dry?

NO!

TEAM

Maya runs like lightning,
but she cannot kick the ball.
Kumar kicks like dynamite,
but he won't pass at all.

Though JJ's great at passing,
he soon runs out of steam.
So it surprises all of us
we make an awesome team.

SALAD DRESSING

I'm mixing up a recipe
to make the greens taste good.
It starts with oil and vinegar
as all good dressings should.

I add some salt and pepper
and then shake it—this is fun.
I float one leaf of lettuce in it.
Now my salad's done!

MUD

Sprayed out a rainbow,
water caused a flood.
Mixed with the dirt,
made slippery mud.

Slid in the puddle,
fell on my bum!
Got a little dirty—
don't tell Mum!

CHOCOLATE MILK

Today we've planned a bash for Mom,
she's turning "umpty-three."
I'm going to make her chocolate milk
instead of boring tea.

Chocolate swirled in fresh white milk
stirred smooth—that makes it best.
This little glass seems right for Mom,
and I will have the rest!

GREEN

Let's decorate Mikey
for Halloween.
We can make him a Martian—
he'll need to be green.

I've only got blue paint,
But—look—you've got yellow.
Hey! Martians are grumpy!
He's starting to bellow.

GOODNIGHT

Just one more glass of water,
and one more time to pee,
and one more check beneath the bed
for monsters—wait with me.

You have to read a story
before you hug me tight.
And then I need a goodnight kiss,
but don't turn off the light!

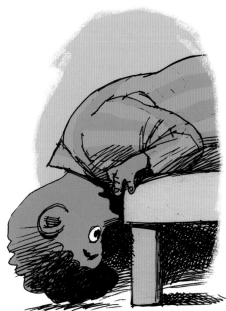

AFTERWORD

These poems are meant, first of all, to be fun and funny. They are also meant to teach young people about the concept of taking two or more substances and simply mixing them together. Most mixtures are not more than the sum of the original elements. Mixing an ice cream with sand from the beach, for example, creates sticky sand. But sometimes the mixture creates something surprisingly different.

Based on the chemistry definition of a mixture, the combined ingredients can be separated afterward. For example, salt dissolved in water is a mixture, and can be separated by evaporating the water, which leaves only the salt. Most, but not all, mixtures in this book follow that definition. Fudge and glue are mixtures, but not in the chemistry sense. Because of chemical reactions that occur during the mixing, the ingredients can't be separated afterward. We've also included abstract mixtures, like music, formed when the band members mix the sounds of the instruments. Goodnight stretches the definition of mixture, because it's a sequence of rituals. But we like the poem a lot, so we included it anyway.

Some of these mixtures will already be familiar to young people. We think it would be fun to make some that are not. We're thinking more of cinnamon toast, bubbles, and green, and not so much of concrete. And making fudge should definitely not be limited to a one-time experience. Most of all, we hope that parents, teachers, and caregivers will read these poems aloud to young people, and that you will all have fun with it.

Simon and Sheryl